Tackylocks

AND THE THREE BEARS

HELEN LESTER

Illustrated by LYNN MUNSINGER

Houghton Mifflin Company Boston 2002

Walter Lorraine Books

To Mary Evelyn Bruce — artist and educator who
brings every stage to life   H. L.

Walter Lorraine (wᴸ) Books

Text copyright © 2002 by Helen Lester
Illustrations copyright © 2002 by Lynn Munsinger

www.houghtonmifflinbooks.com

Library of Congress Cataloging-in-Publication Data

Lester, Helen.
  Tackylocks and the three bears / Helen Lester ; illustrated by Lynn
Munsinger.
     p. cm.
Summary: Takcy the penguin and his friends perform a play for the little
penguins in Mrs. Beakly's class, but with Tacky in the lead role, things
do not go exactly as planned.
  ISBN 0-618-22490-4
  [1. School plays—Fiction. 2. Schools—Fiction. 3. Penguins—Fiction.]
I. Munsinger, Lynn, ill. II. Title.
  PZ7.L56285 Tabf 2002
  [E]—dc21
                                                            2002001477

Printed in the United States of America
WOZ 10 9 8 7 6 5 4 3 2 1

In a nice, icy land, something was happening.

"WHAT'S HAPPENING?" blared Tacky the Penguin as he came
across his companions Goodly, Lovely, Angel, Neatly, and Perfect.
"A play," they replied. "That's what's happening."
"PLAY!" shrieked Tacky in delight. "PLAY!
Love it, love it, love it!"

He waddled off at full speed and was back in a moment.
"I'm ready!"

"No, Tacky, a play. We're going to perform a play
about the three bears for Mrs. Beakly's school."

"Now first we must each choose a part."
"A part of what?" wondered Tacky.

To choose a part, each penguin put a flipper into a bowl
and drew out a piece of paper.

Goodly and Lovely were proud to be announcers.

Angel, Neatly, and Perfect were pleased to be the three bears.

And Tacky . . .

7

For a whole week Goodly, Lovely, Angel, Neatly, and Perfect practiced their lines.

"WELCOME TO OUR PLAY."

"SOMEONE'S TAKEN A WEE NIBBLE OF MY PORRIDGE."

"SOMEONE'S BEEN SITTING IN MY CHAIR."

"SOMEONE'S BEEN SLEEPING IN MY BED."

"THIS ENDS OUR PLAY."

Tacky practiced his lines, too.

At last the day of the play arrived.
The penguin players, even Tacky, knew their lines by heart, but this time it would be the real thing.

With real costumes.

And real porridge.

And real chairs.

And real-looking beds.

Right on time the audience arrived and took their seats.

Sort of.

"WELCOME TO OUR PLAY,"
announced Goodly.
No one listened.

"WELCOME TO OUR PLAY,"
he tried again in a louder voice.

"WELCOME TO OUR . . .
oh, never mind."

"Looks like we have a tough audience," said Goodly.
Everyone was nervous.

Almost everyone.

Onto the stage waddled the three penguin bears
to do their official song and dance:

"WE'RE BEARS WITHOUT HAIRS
BUT WHO REALLY CARES?
WE'RE SMART.
AND THIS IS ART.
SO THERES."

Then it was Tacky's turn.

He skipped onstage and right into the table.
He hadn't tried his skipping shoes before.
"Ooooooo, it's TACKYLOCKS!" cried the audience.

In a loud and clear voice Tacky spoke his lines.
"THIS PORRIDGE IS TOO HOT."
But he ate it anyway.

"THIS PORRIDGE IS TOO COLD."
But he ate it anyway.

"AND THIS PORRIDGE IS JUST RIGHT."
With the just right porridge he had no choice.
He ate it.
Mmmmmmm.

Now, thought Tacky, *if only I could find a little something for dessert. It would only take a moment. Perhaps there might be just the right something up in the cabinet.*
Tacky dragged over the biggest chair.
He put the middle-sized
chair on the big chair, put
the little chair on the middle-sized
chair, climbed to the top,
stood on tiptoe, and . . .

A penguin full of porridge does not fall like a snowflake.
"Cool!" cheered the little fuzzy ones.

Tacky felt lucky that the next scene was in the bedroom,
because a little rest would feel good.
Thinking cozy thoughts, he waddled to the big bed. It
was too hard, for it was merely a stage bed, and beneath
the covers it was only a pile of ice blocks.

"THIS BED IS TOO HARD," said Tackylocks, and he went
to the middle-sized bed.

"THIS BED IS TOO SOFT."
It too was only a stage bed, and
under the covers was a rubber raft.

So Tackylocks rolled all of the bedding over to the little bed.
The little bed was a real bed.

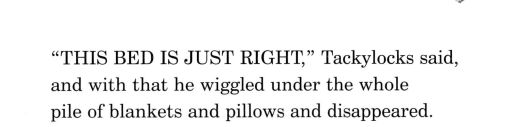

"THIS BED IS JUST RIGHT," Tackylocks said,
and with that he wiggled under the whole
pile of blankets and pillows and disappeared.

"WE'RE HOME AND HUNGRY AS BEARS,"
announced the three bears as
they marched onstage.
Papa bear held the large empty bowl
and cried, "SOMEONE HAS TAKEN
A LITTLE TASTE OF MY PORRIDGE."

"AND A TINY NIBBLE OF MINE," added
Mama, holding another very
empty bowl.

Baby bear wailed, "YOU THINK YOU
HAVE TROUBLE? MY PORRIDGE IS ALL GONE!"
This sounded pretty silly, since
he wasn't the only one with an empty bowl.

"WE NEED TO SIT IN OUR CHAIRS AND DISCUSS THIS,"
said the three bears.
Papa bear said, "SOMEONE HAS BEEN SITTING IN MY . . .
where? Chair?"
Mama bear said, "SOMEONE HAS BEEN SITTING IN MY . . .
wait a minute."
Baby bear said, "SOMEONE HAS BEEN . . . oh, never mind."

This play was not going at all as they had planned.

The frazzled bears marched to the bedroom.
"SOMEONE HAS BEEN SLEEPING IN MY . . . um, pile of ice blocks,"
growled Papa bear.
"SOMEONE HAS BEEN SLEEPING IN MY . . . uh, rubber raft, too,"
added Mama.

And Baby bear squealed, "SOMEONE HAS BEEN SLEEPING IN MY BED, AND THAT SOMEONE'S STILL THERE! I hope." The three penguins dug desperately. Where could Tacky be? Finally Baby bear cried, "I've got it by the beak!"

The bears threw pillows to and fro until all of Tacky
appeared and shouted, "PILLOW FIGHT!"

"Hooray!" yelled the audience.

Feathers flew everywhere until everyone was exhausted.
"Looks like our play has ended, Tacky," said Goodly, Lovely,
Angel, Neatly, and Perfect.

Just then Mrs. Beakly arrived to pick up her class.
"And how did you like the play, children?" she asked.
"Best play ever! Hooray for Tackylocks!" they cheered.

Tackylocks was an odd bird, but a nice bird to have around.